# THE SPY

## BY

## RICHARD HARDING DAVIS

**British Library Cataloguing-in-Publication Data**
A catalogue record for this book is available from the
British Library

# Richard Harding Davis

Richard Harding Davis was born on 18th April 1864, in Philadelphia, Pennsylvania. He was the son of two writers, Rebecca Harding Davis (a prominent author), and Lemuel Clarke Davis (a journalist and editor of the Philadelphia Public Ledger).

Davis attended Lehigh University and Johns Hopkins University, but was asked to leave both due to neglecting his studies in favour socialising. With some help from his father, Davis was able to find a position as a journalist at the Philadelphia Record, but was soon fired from the post. He then spent a short time at the Philadelphia Press before moving to the New York Evening Sun, where he became a controversial figure, writing on subjects such as execution, abortion, and suicide. He went on to edit Harper's Weekly and write for the New York Herald, The Times, and Scribner's Magazine.

During the Second Boer War in South Africa, Davis was a leading correspondent of the conflict. He saw the war first-hand from both parties perspectives and documented it in his publication With Both Armies (1900). Later in his career he wrote a story about his experience on a United States Navy ship that shelled Cuba as part of the Battle of Santiago de Cuba. His article made the headlines and prompted the

Navy to refuse to allow reporters aboard their vessels for the remainder of the war.

He wrote widely from locations such as the Caribbean, Central America, and even from the perspective of the Japanese forces during the Russo-Japanese War. He also covered the Salonika Front in the First World War, where he spent a time detained by the Germans on suspicion of being a spy.

Davis married twice, first to Cecil Clark in 1899, and then to Bessie McCoy in 1912, with whom he had one daughter. Davis died following a heart attack on 11th April, 1916, at the age of 51.

My going to Valencia was entirely an accident. But the more often I stated that fact, the more satisfied was everyone at the capital that I had come on some secret mission. Even the venerable politician who acted as our minister, the night of my arrival, after dinner, said confidentially, "Now, Mr. Crosby, between ourselves, what's the game?"

"What's what game?" I asked.

"You know what I mean," he returned. "What are you here for?"

But when, for the tenth time, I repeated how I came to be marooned in Valencia he showed that his feelings were hurt, and said stiffly: "As you please. Suppose we join the ladies."

And the next day his wife reproached me with: "I should think you could trust your own minister. My husband NEVER talks—not even to me."

"So I see," I said.

And then her feelings were hurt also, and she went about telling people I was an agent of the Walker-Keefe crowd.

My only reason for repeating here that my going to Valencia was an accident is that it was because Schnitzel disbelieved that fact, and to drag the hideous facts from me followed me back to New York. Through that circumstance I came to know him, and am able to tell his story.

The simple truth was that I had been sent by the State Department to Panama to "go, look, see," and straighten out a certain conflict of authority among the officials of the canal zone. While I was there the yellow-fever broke out, and every self-respecting power clapped a quarantine on the Isthmus, with the result that when I tried to return to New York no steamer would take me to any place to which any white man would care to go. But I knew that at Valencia there was a direct line to New York, so I took a tramp steamer down the coast to Valencia. I went to Valencia only because to me every other port in the world was closed. My position was that of the man who explained to his wife that he came home because the other places were shut.

But, because, formerly in Valencia I had held a minor post in our legation, and because the State Department so constantly consults our firm on questions of international law, it was believed I revisited Valencia on some mysterious and secret mission.

As a matter of fact, had I gone there to sell phonographs or to start a steam laundry, I should have been as greatly suspected. For in Valencia even every commercial salesman, from the moment he gives up his passport on the steamer until the police permit him to depart, is suspected, shadowed, and begirt with spies.

I believe that during my brief visit I enjoyed the distinction of occupying the undivided attention of three: a common or garden Government spy, from whom no guilty man escapes, a Walker-Keefe spy, and the spy of the Nitrate Company. The spy of the Nitrate Company is generally a man you meet at the legations and clubs. He plays bridge and is dignified with the title of "agent." The Walker-Keefe spy is ostensibly a travelling salesman or hotel runner. The Government spy is just a spy—a scowling, important little beast in a white duck suit and a diamond ring. The limit of his intelligence is to follow you into a cigar store and note what cigar you buy, and in what kind of money you pay for it.

The reason for it all was the three-cornered fight which then was being waged by the Government, the Nitrate Trust, and the Walker-Keefe crowd for the possession of the nitrate beds. Valencia is so near to the equator, and so far from New York, that there are few who studied the intricate story of that disgraceful struggle, which, I hasten to add, with the fear of libel before my eyes, I do not intend to tell now.

Briefly, it was a triangular fight between opponents each of whom was in the wrong, and each of whom, to gain his end, bribed, blackmailed, and robbed, not only his adversaries, but those of his own side, the end in view being the possession of those great deposits that lie in the rocks of Valencia, baked from above by the tropic sun and from below by volcanic fires. As one of their engineers, one night in the Plaza, said to me: "Those mines were conceived in hell, and stink to heaven, and the reputation of every man of us that has touched them smells like the mines."

At the time I was there the situation was "acute." In Valencia the situation always is acute, but this time it looked as though something might happen. On the day before I departed the Nitrate Trust had cabled vehemently for war-ships, the Minister of Foreign Affairs had refused to receive our minister, and at Porto Banos a mob had made the tin sign of the United States consulate look like a sieve. Our minister urged me to remain. To be bombarded by one's own war-ships, he assured me, would be a thrilling experience.

But I repeated that my business was with Panama, not Valencia, and that if in this matter of his row I had any weight at Washington, as between preserving the nitrate beds for the trust, and preserving for his country and various sweethearts one brown-throated, clean-limbed bluejacket, I was for the bluejacket.

Accordingly, when I sailed from Valencia the aged diplomat would have described our relations as strained.

Our ship was a slow ship, listed to touch at many ports, and as early as noon on the following day we stopped for cargo at Trujillo. It was there I met Schnitzel.

In Panama I had bought a macaw for a little niece of mine, and while we were taking on cargo I went ashore to get a tin cage in which to put it, and, for direction, called upon our consul. From an inner room he entered excitedly, smiling at my card, and asked how he might serve me. I told him I had a parrot below decks, and wanted to buy a tin cage.

"Exactly. You want a tin cage," the consul repeated soothingly. "The State Department doesn't keep me awake nights cabling me what it's going to do," he said, "but at least I know it doesn't send a thousand-dollar-a-minute, four-cylinder lawyer all the way to this fever swamp to buy a tin cage. Now, honest, how can I serve you?" I saw it was hopeless. No one would believe the truth. To offer it to this friendly soul would merely offend his feelings and his intelligence.

So, with much mystery, I asked him to describe the "situation," and he did so with the exactness of one who believes that within an hour every word he speaks will be cabled to the White House.

When I was leaving he said: "Oh, there's a newspaper correspondent after you. He wants an interview, I guess. He followed you last night from the capital by train. You want to watch out he don't catch you. His name is Jones." I promised to be on my guard against a man named Jones, and the consul escorted me to the ship. As he went down the accommodation ladder, I called over the rail: "In case they SHOULD declare war, cable to Curacoa, and I'll come back. And don't cable anything indefinite, like 'Situation critical' or 'War imminent.' Understand? Cable me, 'Come back' or 'Go ahead.' But whatever you cable, make it CLEAR."

He shook his head violently and with his green-lined umbrella pointed at my elbow. I turned and found a young man hungrily listening to my words. He was leaning on the rail with his chin on his arms and the brim of his Panama hat drawn down to conceal his eyes.

On the pier-head, from which we now were drawing rapidly away, the consul made a megaphone of his hands.

"That's HIM," he called. "That's Jones."

Jones raised his head, and I saw that the tropical heat had made Jones thirsty, or that with friends he had been celebrating his departure. He winked at me, and, apparently with pleasure at his own discernment and with pity for me, smiled.

"Oh, of course!" he murmured. His tone was one of heavy irony. "Make it 'clear.' Make it clear to the whole wharf. Shout it out so's everybody can hear you. You're 'clear' enough." His disgust was too deep for ordinary words. "My uncle!" he exclaimed.

By this I gathered that he was expressing his contempt.

"I beg your pardon?" I said.

We had the deck to ourselves. Its emptiness suddenly reminded me that we had the ship, also, to ourselves. I remembered the purser had told me that, except for those who travelled overnight from port to port, I was his only passenger.

With dismay I pictured myself for ten days adrift on the high seas—alone with Jones.

With a dramatic gesture, as one would say, "I am here!" he pushed back his Panama hat. With an unsteady finger he pointed, as it was drawn dripping across the deck, at the stern hawser.

"You see that rope?" he demanded. "Soon as that rope hit the water I knocked off work. S'long as you was in Valencia—me, on the job. Now, YOU can't go back, I can't go back. Why further dissim'lation? WHO AM I?"

His condition seemed to preclude the possibility of his knowing who he was, so I told him.

He sneered as I have seen men sneer only in melodrama.

"Oh, of course," he muttered. "Oh, of course."

He lurched toward me indignantly.

"You know perfec'ly well Jones is not my name. You know perfec'ly well who I am."

"My dear sir," I said, "I don't know anything about you, except that your are a damned nuisance."

He swayed from me, pained and surprised. Apparently he was upon an outbreak of tears.

"Proud," he murmured, "AND haughty. Proud and haughty to the last."

I never have understood why an intoxicated man feels the climax of insult is to hurl at you your name. Perhaps because he knows it is the one charge you cannot deny. But invariably before you escape, as though assured the words will cover your retreat with shame, he throws at you your full title. Jones did this.

Slowly and mercilessly he repeated, "Mr.—George—Morgan—Crosby. Of Harvard," he added. "Proud and haughty to the last."

He then embraced a passing steward, and demanded to be informed why the ship rolled. He never knew a ship to roll as our ship rolled.

"Perfec'ly satisfact'ry ocean, but ship—rolling like a stone-breaker. Take me some place in the ship where this ship don't roll."

The steward led him away.

When he had dropped the local pilot the captain beckoned me to the bridge.

"I saw you talking to Mr. Schnitzel," he said. "He's a little under the weather. He has too light a head for liquors."

I agreed that he had a light head, and said I understood his name was Jones.

"That's what I wanted to tell you," said the captain. "His name is Schnitzel. He used to work for the Nitrate Trust in New York. Then he came down here as an agent. He's a good boy not to tell things to. Understand? Sometimes I carry

10

him under one name, and the next voyage under another. The purser and he fix it up between 'em. It pleases him, and it don't hurt anybody else, so long as I tell them about it. I don't know who he's working for now," he went on, "but I know he's not with the Nitrate Company any more. He sold them out."

"How could he?" I asked. "He's only a boy."

"He had a berth as typewriter to Senator Burnsides, president of the Nitrate Trust, sort of confidential stenographer," said the captain. "Whenever the senator dictated an important letter, they say, Schnitzel used to make a carbon copy, and when he had enough of them he sold them to the Walker-Keefe crowd. Then, when Walker-Keefe lost their suit in the Valencia Supreme Court I guess Schnitzel went over to President Alvarez. And again, some folks say he's back with the Nitrate Company."

"After he sold them out?"

"Yes, but you see he's worth more to them now. He knows all the Walker-Keefe secrets and Alvarez's secrets, too."

I expressed my opinion of every one concerned.

"It shouldn't surprise YOU," complained the captain. "You know the country. Every man in it is out for something that isn't his. The pilot wants his bit, the health doctor must get his, the customs take all your cigars, and if you don't put up gold for the captain of the port and the alcalde and the commandant and the harbor police and the foreman of the cargadores, they won't move a lighter, and they'll hold up the ship's papers. Well, an American comes down here, honest and straight and willing to work for his wages. But pretty quick he finds every one is getting his squeeze but him, so he tries to get some of it back by robbing the natives that robbed him. Then he robs the other foreigners, and it ain't long before he's cheating the people at home who sent him here. There isn't a man in this nitrate row that isn't robbing the crowd he's with, and that wouldn't change sides for money. Schnitzel's no worse than the president nor the canteen contractor."

He waved his hand at the glaring coast-line, at the steaming swamps and the hot, naked mountains.

"It's the country that does it," he said. "It's in the air. You can smell it as soon as you drop anchor, like you smell the slaughter-house at Punta-Arenas."

"How do YOU manage to keep honest," I asked, smiling.

"I don't take any chances," exclaimed the captain seriously. "When I'm in their damned port I don't go ashore."

I did not again see Schnitzel until, with haggard eyes and suspiciously wet hair, he joined the captain, doctor, purser, and myself at breakfast. In the phrases of the Tenderloin, he told us cheerfully that he had been grandly intoxicated, and to recover drank mixtures of raw egg, vinegar, and red pepper, the sight of which took away every appetite save his own. When to this he had added a bottle of beer, he declared himself a new man. The new man followed me to the deck, and with the truculent bearing of one who expects to be repelled, he asked if, the day before, he had not made a fool of himself.

I suggested he had been somewhat confidential. At once he recovered his pose and patronized me.

"Don't you believe it," he said. "That's all part of my game. 'Confidence for confidence' is the way I work it. That's how I learn things. I tell a man something on the inside, and he says: 'Here's a nice young fellow. Nothing standoffish about him,' and he tells me something he shouldn't. Like as not what I told him wasn't true. See?"

I assured him he interested me greatly.

"You find, then, in your line of business," I asked, "that apparent frankness is advisable? As a rule," I explained, "secrecy is what a—a person in your line—a—"

To save his feelings I hesitated at the word.

"A spy," he said. His face beamed with fatuous complacency.

"But if I had not known you were a spy," I asked, "would not that have been better for you?"

"In dealing with a party like you, Mr. Crosby," Schnitzel began sententiously, "I use a different method. You're on a secret mission yourself, and you get your information about the nitrate row one way, and I get it another. I deal with you just like we were drummers in the same line of goods. We are rivals in business, but outside of business hours perfect gentleman."

In the face of the disbelief that had met my denials of any secret mission, I felt to have Schnitzel also disbelieve me would be too great a humiliation. So I remained silent.

"You make your report to the State Department," he explained, "and I make mine to—my people. Who they are doesn't matter. You'd like to know, and I don't want to hurt your feelings, but—that's MY secret."

My only feelings were a desire to kick Schnitzel heavily, but for Schnitzel to suspect that was impossible. Rather, he pictured me as shaken by his disclosures.

As he hung over the rail the glare of the sun on the tumbling water lit up his foolish, mongrel features, exposed their cunning, their utter lack of any character, and showed behind the shifty eyes the vacant, half-crooked mind.

Schnitzel was smiling to himself with a smile of complete self-satisfaction. In the light of his later conduct, I grew to understand that smile. He had anticipated a rebuff, and he had been received, as he read it, with consideration. The irony of my politeness he had entirely missed. Instead, he read in what I said the admiration of the amateur for the professional. He saw what he believed to be a high agent of the Government treating him as a worthy antagonist. In no other way can I explain his later heaping upon me his confidences. It was the vanity of a child trying to show off.

In ten days, in the limited area of a two-thousand-ton steamer, one could not help but learn something of the history of so communicative a fellow-passenger as Schnitzel. His parents were German and still lived in Germany. But he himself had been brought up on the East Side. An uncle who kept a delicatessen shop in Avenue A had sent him to the public schools and then to a "business college," where he had developed remarkable expertness as a stenographer. He referred to his skill in this difficult exercise with pitying contempt. Nevertheless, from a room noisy with type-writers this skill had lifted him into the private office of the president of the Nitrate Trust. There, as Schnitzel expressed it, "I saw 'mine,' and I took it." To trace back the criminal instinct that led Schnitzel to steal and sell the private letters of his employer was not difficult. In all of his few early years I found it lying latent. Of every story he told of himself, and he talked only of himself, there was not one that was not to his discredit. He himself never saw this, nor that all he told me showed he was without the moral sense, and with an instinctive enjoyment of what was deceitful, mean, and underhand. That, as I read it, was his character.

In appearance he was smooth-shaven, with long locks that hung behind wide, protruding ears. He had the unhealthy skin of bad blood, and his eyes, as though the daylight hurt them, constantly opened and shut. He was like hundreds of young men that you see loitering on upper Broadway and making predatory raids along the Rialto. Had you passed him in that neighborhood you would have set him down as a wire-tapper, a racing tout, a would-be actor.

As I worked it out, Schnitzel was a spy because it gave him an importance he had not been able to obtain by any other effort. As a child and as a clerk, it was easy to see that among his associates Schnitzel must always have been the butt. Until suddenly, by one dirty action, he had placed himself outside their class. As he expressed it: "Whenever I walk through the office now, where all the stenographers sit, you ought to see those slobs look after me. When they go to the president's door, they got to knock, like I used to, but now, when the old man sees me coming to make my report after one of these trips he calls out, 'Come right in, Mr. Schnitzel.' And like as not I go in with my hat on and offer him a cigar. An' they see me do it, too!"

To me, that speech seemed to give Schnitzel's view of the values of his life. His vanity demanded he be pointed at, if even with contempt. But the contempt never reached him—he only knew that at last people took note of him. They no longer laughed at him, they were afraid of him. In his heart he believed that they regarded him as one who walked in the dark places of world politics, who possessed an evil knowledge of great men as evil as himself, as one who by blackmail held public ministers at his mercy.

This view of himself was the one that he tried to give me. I probably was the first decent man who ever had treated him civilly, and to impress me with his knowledge he spread that knowledge before me. It was sale, shocking, degrading.

At first I took comfort in the thought that Schnitzel was a liar. Later, I began to wonder if all of it were a lie, and finally, in a way I could not doubt, it was proved to me that the worst he charged was true.

The night I first began to believe him was the night we touched at Cristobal, the last port in Valencia. In the most light-hearted manner he had been accusing all concerned in the nitrate fight with every crime known in Wall Street and in the dark reaches of the Congo River.

"But, I know him, Mr. Schnitzel," I said sternly. "He is incapable of it. I went to college with him."

"I don't care whether he's a rah-rah boy or not," said Schnitzel, "I know that's what he did when he was up the Orinoco after orchids, and if the tribe had ever caught him they'd have crucified him. And I know this, too: he made forty thousand dollars out of the Nitrate Company on a ten-thousand-dollar job. And I know it, because he beefed to me about it himself, because it wasn't big enough."

We were passing the limestone island at the entrance to the harbor, where, in the prison fortress, with its muzzle-loading guns pointing drunkenly at the sky, are buried the political prisoners of Valencia.

"Now, there," said Schnitzel, pointing, "that shows you what the Nitrate Trust can do. Judge Rojas is in there. He gave the first decision in favor of the Walker-Keefe people, and for making that decision William T. Scott, the Nitrate manager, made Alvarez put Rojas in there. He's seventy years old, and he's been there five years. The cell they keep him in is below the sea-level, and the salt-water leaks through the wall. I've seen it. That's what William T. Scott did, an' up in New York people think 'Billy' Scott is a fine man. I seen him at the Horse Show sitting in a box, bowing to everybody, with his wife sitting beside him, all hung out with pearls. An' that was only a month after I'd seen Rojas in that sewer where Scott put him."

"Schnitzel," I laughed, "you certainly are a magnificent liar."

Schnitzel showed no resentment.

"Go ashore and look for yourself," he muttered. "Don't believe me. Ask Rojas. Ask the first man you meet." He shivered, and shrugged his shoulders. "I tell you, the walls are damp, like sweat."

The Government had telegraphed the commandant to come on board and, as he expressed it, "offer me the hospitality of the port," which meant that I had to take him to the smoking-room and give him champagne. What the

Government really wanted was to find out whether I was still on board, and if it were finally rid of me.

I asked the official concerning Judge Rojas.

"Oh, yes," he said readily. "He is still incomunicado."

Without believing it would lead to anything, I suggested:

"It was foolish of him to give offence to Mr. Scott?"

The commandant nodded vivaciously.

"Mr. Scott is very powerful man," he assented. "We all very much love Mr. Scott. The president, he love Mr. Scott, too, but the judges were not sympathetic to Mr. Scott, so Mr. Scott asked our president to give them a warning, and Senor Rojas—he is the warning."

"When will he get out?" I asked.

The commandant held up the glass in the sunlight from the open air-port, and gazed admiringly at the bubbles.

"Who can tell," he said. "Any day when Mr. Scott wishes. Maybe, never. Senor Rojas is an old man. Old, and he has much rheumatics. Maybe, he will never come out to see our beloved country any more."

As we left the harbor we passed so close that one could throw a stone against the wall of the fortress. The sun was just sinking and the air became suddenly chilled. Around the little island of limestone the waves swept through the sea-weed and black manigua up to the rusty bars of the cells. I saw the barefooted soldiers smoking upon the sloping ramparts, the common criminals in a long stumbling line bearing kegs of water, three storm-beaten palms rising like gallows, and the green and yellow flag of Valencia crawling down the staff. Somewhere entombed in that blotched and mildewed masonry an old man of seventy years was shivering and hugging himself from the damp and cold. A man who spoke five languages, a just, brave gentleman. To me it was no new story. I knew of the horrors of Cristobal prison; of political rivals chained to criminals loathsome with disease, of men who had raised the flag of revolution driven to suicide. But never had I supposed that my own people could reach from the city of New York and cast a fellow-man into that cellar of fever and madness.

As I watched the yellow wall sink into the sea, I became conscious that Schnitzel was near me, as before, leaning on the rail, with his chin sunk on his arms. His face was turned toward the fortress, and for the first time since I had known him it was set and serious. And when, a moment later, he passed me without recognition, I saw that his eyes were filled with fear.

When we touched at Curacoa I sent a cable to my sister, announcing the date of my arrival, and then continued on to the Hotel Venezuela. Almost immediately Schnitzel joined me. With easy carelessness he said: "I was in the cable office just now, sending off a wire, and that operator told me he can't make head or tail of the third word in your cable."

"That is strange," I commented, "because it's a French word, and he is French. That's why I wrote it in French."

With the air of one who nails another in a falsehood, Schnitzel exclaimed:

"Then, how did you suppose your sister was going to read it? It's a cipher, that's what it is. Oh, no, YOU'RE not on a secret mission! Not at all!"

It was most undignified of me, but in five minutes I excused myself, and sent to the State Department the following words:

"Roses red, violets blue, send snow."

Later at the State Department the only person who did not eventually pardon my jest was the clerk who had sat up until three in the morning with my cable, trying to fit it to any known code.

Immediately after my return to the Hotel Venezuela Schnitzel excused himself, and half an hour later returned in triumph with the cable operator and ordered lunch for both. They imbibed much sweet champagne.

When we again were safe at sea, I said: "Schnitzel, how much did you pay that Frenchman to let you read my second cable?"

Schnitzel's reply was prompt and complacent.

"One hundred dollars gold. It was worth it. Do you want to know how I doped it out?"

I even challenged him to do so. "'Roses red'—war declared; 'violets blue'—outlook bad, or blue; 'send snow'—send squadron, because the white squadron is white like snow. See? It was too easy."

"Schnitzel," I cried, "you are wonderful!"

Schnitzel yawned in my face.

"Oh, you don't have to hit the soles of my feet with a night-stick to keep me awake," he said.

After I had been a week at sea, I found that either I had to believe that in all things Schnitzel was a liar, or that the men of the Nitrate Trust were in all things evil. I was convinced that instead of the people of Valencia robbing them, they were robbing both the people of Valencia and the people of the United States.

To go to war on their account was to degrade our Government. I explained to Schnitzel it was not becoming that the United States navy should be made the cat's-paw of a corrupt corporation. I asked his permission to repeat to the authorities at Washington certain of the statements he had made.

Schnitzel was greatly pleased.

"You're welcome to tell 'em anything I've said," he assented. "And," he added, "most of it's true, too."

I wrote down certain charges he had made, and added what I had always known of the nitrate fight. It was a terrible arraignment. In the evening I read my notes to Schnitzel, who, in a corner of the smoking-room, sat, frowning importantly, checking off each statement, and where I made an error of a date or a name, severely correcting me.

Several times I asked him, "Are you sure this won't get you into trouble with your 'people'? You seem to accuse everybody on each side."

Schnitzel's eyes instantly closed with suspicion.

"Don't you worry about me and my people," he returned sulkily. "That's MY secret, and you won't find it out, neither. I may be as crooked as the rest of them, but I'm not giving away my employer."

I suppose I looked puzzled.

"I mean not a second time," he added hastily. "I know what you're thinking of, and I got five thousand dollars for it. But now I mean to stick by the men that pay my wages."

"But you've told me enough about each of the three to put any one of them in jail."

"Of course, I have," cried Schnitzel triumphantly.

"If I'd let down on any one crowd you'd know I was working for that crowd, so I've touched 'em all up. Only what I told you about my crowd—isn't true."

The report we finally drew up was so sensational that I was of a mind to throw it overboard. It accused members of the Cabinet, of our Senate, diplomats, business men of national interest, judges of the Valencia courts, private secretaries, clerks, hired bullies, and filibusters. Men the trust could not bribe it had blackmailed. Those it could not corrupt, and they were pitifully few, it crushed with some disgraceful charge.

Looking over my notes, I said:

"You seem to have made every charge except murder."

"How'd I come to leave that out?" Schnitzel answered flippantly. "What about Coleman, the foreman at Bahia, and that German contractor, Ebhardt, and old Smedburg? They talked too much, and they died of yellow-fever, maybe, and maybe what happened to them was they ate knockout drops in their soup."

I disbelieved him, but there came a sudden nasty doubt.

"Curtis, who managed the company's plant at Barcelona, died of yellow-fever," I said, "and was buried the same day."

For some time Schnitzel glowered uncertainly at the bulkhead.

"Did you know him?" he asked.

"When I was in the legation I knew him well," I said.

"So did I," said Schnitzel. "He wasn't murdered. He murdered himself. He was wrong ten thousand dollars in his accounts. He got worrying about it and we found him outside the clearing with a hole in his head. He left a note saying he couldn't bear the disgrace. As if the company would hold a little grafting against as good a man as Curtis!"

Schnitzel coughed and pretended it was his cigarette.

"You see you don't put in nothing against him," he added savagely.

It was the first time I had seen Schnitzel show emotion, and I was moved to preach.

"Why don't you quit?" I said. "You had an A-1 job as a stenographer. Why don't you go back to it?"

"Maybe, some day. But it's great being your own boss. If I was a stenographer, I wouldn't be helping you send in a report to the State Department, would I? No, this job is all right. They send you after something big, and you have the devil of a time getting it, but when you get it, you feel like you had picked a hundred-to-one shot."

The talk or the drink had elated him. His fish-like eyes bulged and shone. He cast a quick look about him. Except for ourselves, the smoking-room was empty. From below came the steady throb of the engines, and from outside the whisper of the waves and of the wind through the cordage. A barefooted sailor pattered by to the bridge. Schnitzel bent toward me, and with his hand pointed to his throat.

"I've got papers on me that's worth a million to a certain party," he whispered. "You understand, my notes in cipher."

He scowled with intense mystery.

"I keep 'em in an oiled-silk bag, tied around my neck with a string. And here," he added hastily, patting his hip, as though to forestall any attack I might make upon his person,

"I carry my automatic. It shoots nine bullets in five seconds. They got to be quick to catch me."

"Well, if you have either of those things on you," I said testily, "I don't want to know it. How often have I told you not to talk and drink at the same time?"

"Ah, go on," laughed Schnitzel. "That's an old gag, warning a fellow not to talk so as to MAKE him talk. I do that myself."

That Schnitzel had important papers tied to his neck I no more believe than that he wore a shirt of chain armor, but to please him I pretended to be greatly concerned.

"Now that we're getting into New York," I said, "you must be very careful. A man who carries such important documents on his person might be murdered for them. I think you ought to disguise yourself."

A picture of my bag being carried ashore by Schnitzel in the uniform of a ship's steward rather pleased me.

"Go on, you're kidding!" said Schnitzel. He was drawn between believing I was deeply impressed and with fear that I was mocking him.

"On the contrary," I protested, "I don't feel quite safe myself. Seeing me with you they may think I have papers around MY neck."

"They wouldn't look at you," Schnitzel reassured me. "They know you're just an amateur. But, as you say, with me, it's different. I GOT to be careful. Now, you mightn't believe it, but I never go near my uncle nor none of my friends that live where I used to hang out. If I did, the other spies would get on my track. I suppose," he went on grandly, "I never go out in New York but that at least two spies are trailing me. But I know how to throw them off. I live 'way down town in a little hotel you never heard of. You never catch me dining at Sherry's nor the Waldorf. And you never met me out socially, did you, now?"

I confessed I had not.

"And then, I always live under an assumed name."

"Like 'Jones'?" I suggested.

"Well, sometimes 'Jones'," he admitted.

"To me," I said, "'Jones' lacks imagination. It's the sort of name you give when you're arrested for exceeding the speed limit. Why don't you call yourself Machiavelli?"

"Go on, I'm no dago," said Schnitzel, "and don't you go off thinking 'Jones' is the only disguise I use. But I'm not tellin' what it is, am I? Oh, no."

"Schnitzel," I asked, "have you ever been told that you would make a great detective?"

"Cut it out," said Schnitzel. "You've been reading those fairy stories. There's no fly cops nor Pinks could do the work I do. They're pikers compared to me. They chase petty-larceny cases and kick in doors. I wouldn't stoop to what they do. It's being mixed up the way I am with the problems of two governments that catches me." He added magnanimously, "You see something of that yourself."

We left the ship at Brooklyn, and with regret I prepared to bid Schnitzel farewell. Seldom had I met a little beast so offensive, but his vanity, his lies, his moral blindness, made one pity him. And in ten days in the smoking-room together we had had many friendly drinks and many friendly laughs. He was going to a hotel on lower Broadway, and as my cab, on my way uptown, passed the door, I offered him a lift. He appeared to consider the advisability of this, and then, with much by-play of glancing over his shoulder, dived into the front seat and drew down the blinds. "This hotel I am going to is an old-fashioned trap," he explained, "but the clerk is wise to me, understand, and I don't have to sign the register."

As we drew nearer to the hotel, he said: "It's a pity we can't dine out somewheres and go to the theatre, but—you know?"

With almost too much heartiness I hastily agreed it would be imprudent.

"I understand perfectly," I assented. "You are a marked man. Until you get those papers safe in the hands of your 'people,' you must be very cautious."

"That's right," he said. Then he smiled craftily.

"I wonder if you're on yet to which my people are."

I assured him that I had no idea, but that from the avidity with which he had abused them I guessed he was working for the Walker-Keefe crowd.

He both smiled and scowled.

"Don't you wish you knew?" he said. "I've told you a lot of inside stories, Mr. Crosby, but I'll never tell on my pals again. Not me! That's MY secret."

At the door of the hotel he bade me a hasty good-by, and for a few minutes I believed that Schnitzel had passed out of my life forever. Then, in taking account of my belongings, I missed my field-glasses. I remembered that, in order to open a trunk for the customs inspectors, I had handed them to Schnitzel, and that he had hung them over his shoulder. In our haste at parting we both had forgotten them.

I was only a few blocks from the hotel, and I told the man to return.

I inquired for Mr. Schnitzel, and the clerk, who apparently knew him by that name, said he was in his room, number eighty-two.

"But he has a caller with him now," he added. "A gentleman was waiting for him, and's just gone up."

I wrote on my card why I had called, and soon after it had been borne skyward the clerk said: "I guess he'll be able to see you now. That's the party that was calling on him, there."

He nodded toward a man who crossed the rotunda quickly. His face was twisted from us, as though, as he almost ran toward the street, he were reading the advertisements on the wall.

He reached the door, and was lost in the great tide of Broadway.

I crossed to the elevator, and as I stood waiting, it descended with a crash, and the boy who had taken my card flung himself, shrieking, into the rotunda.

"That man—stop him!" he cried. "The man in eighty-two—he's murdered."

The clerk vaulted the desk and sprang into the street, and I dragged the boy back to the wire rope and we shot to the third story. The boy shrank back. A chambermaid, crouching against the wall, her face colorless, lowered one hand, and pointed at an open door.

"In there," she whispered.

In a mean, common room, stretched where he had been struck back upon the bed, I found the boy who had elected to meddle in the "problems of two governments."

In tiny jets, from three wide knife-wounds, his blood flowed slowly. His staring eyes were lifted up in fear and in entreaty. I knew that he was dying, and as I felt my impotence to help him, I as keenly felt a great rage and a hatred toward those who had struck him.

I leaned over him until my eyes were only a few inches from his face.

"Schnitzel!" I cried. "Who did this? You can trust me. Who did this? Quick!"

I saw that he recognized me, and that there was something which, with terrible effort, he was trying to make me understand.

In the hall was the rush of many people, running, exclaiming, the noise of bells ringing; from another floor the voice of a woman shrieked hysterically.

At the sounds the eyes of the boy grew eloquent with entreaty, and with a movement that called from each wound a fresh outburst, like a man strangling, he lifted his fingers to his throat.

Voices were calling for water, to wait for the doctor, to wait for the police. But I thought I understood.

Still doubting him, still unbelieving, ashamed of my own credulity, I tore at his collar, and my fingers closed upon a package of oiled silk.

I stooped, and with my teeth ripped it open, and holding before him the slips of paper it contained, tore them into tiny shreds.

The eyes smiled at me with cunning, with triumph, with deep content.

It was so like the Schnitzel I had known that I believed still he might have strength enough to help me.

"Who did this?" I begged. "I'll hang him for it! Do you hear me?" I cried.

Seeing him lying there, with the life cut out of him, swept me with a blind anger, with a need to punish.

"I'll see they hang for it. Tell me!" I commanded. "Who did this?"

The eyes, now filled with weariness, looked up and the lips moved feebly.

"My own people," he whispered.

In my indignation I could have shaken the truth from him. I bent closer.

"Then, by God," I whispered back, "you'll tell me who they are!"

The eyes flashed sullenly.

"That's my secret," said Schnitzel.

The eyes set and the lips closed.

A man at my side leaned over him, and drew the sheet across his face.

www.ingramcontent.com/pod-product-compliance
Lightning Source LLC
Chambersburg PA
CBHW030242180626
46810CB00008B/3256